For Ethan—T.T.

To Dimitra, Phoebe, and Kyra for their love and support—D.C.

Distributed in the United States by NorthSouth Books, Inc., New York 10016.
Library of Congress Cataloging-in-Publication Data is available.
ISBN: 978-0-7358-4199-4
Printed in China by Leo Paper Products Ltd., Heshan, Guangdong, April 2015.
3 5 7 9 • 10 8 6 4 2
www.northsouth.com

FSC
www.fsc.org
MIX
Paper from
responsible sources
FSC® C020056

My Grandma's a
NINJA

By Todd Tarpley

Illustrated by

Danny Chatzikonstantinou

North
South

My grandma came to visit last week. She's a ninja! It's true. It was fun, at first. . . .

Instead of riding the school bus, we took a zip line. We zipped past the crossing guard so fast, his uniform blew off. All my friends were like, *"Whoa!"*

At show-and-tell Ms. Rotter asked, "What did you bring today, Ethan?"
I said, "A ninja."

Then Grandma dropped from the ceiling, and everyone laughed—except Ms. Rotter. She fainted and took the rest of the day off.

At recess all the big kids wanted to be friends with me.
"Is she a *real* ninja?" they asked. "Can she teach us karate moves?"
"You bet!" I said.

And she did.

On the way home she said we should rub mud all over ourselves and roll in the leaves so that our enemies couldn't track us.

"Good idea!" I said.

But it freaked Mom out. She dropped her favorite vase.
She had to lie down, so we didn't get to go to dinner at
my favorite restaurant like we'd planned.
Grandma made dinner instead. It was raw fish.
It was horrible.

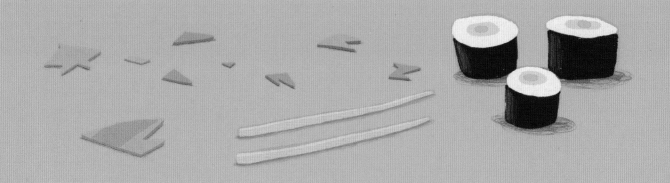

The next day Grandma brought me to soccer practice. My teammates were excited.

"Is she a *real* ninja? Can she flip upside down in slow motion? And freeze in midair?"

"Yeah." I sighed.

And she did.

But when she landed, she kicked the ball so hard that it deflated. *POOF!*

"Soccer practice is over," announced Coach Randall. "Everyone go home."

My teammates were mad.
"Why'd you have to bring your ninja grandma!" they said.
I was mad too.

"No more zip-lining," I told her on the way home. "No more hanging upside down. No more rolling in leaves. And no more deflating soccer balls."

"I'll try," said Grandma. "But I am a ninja, after all."

"Try very hard," I said. "My soccer game is tomorrow, and if you deflate the ball again, we'll lose."

As soon as we got home, she somersaulted across the
lawn, dived through the hedge, and catapulted from a tree
limb into the dark night.

The next day Grandma wasn't there to take me to school.

I took the bus.

At show-and-tell Ms. Rotter asked, "What did you bring today, Ethan?"

Everyone looked up at the ceiling, but Grandma wasn't there.

"Nothing," I said.

Even Ms. Rotter seemed a little disappointed.

At recess no one would play with me. They were still mad
about the soccer ball.

I was still mad too—but mostly I just missed Grandma.
"She can't help being a ninja, you know," I told them.

After school was the big game. Mom and Dad were there.
But not Grandma.

All the players on the other team were bigger and faster.

We were getting creamed.

"Don't give up!" yelled Dad.

"Focus!" yelled Coach Randall.

"NINJA!" yelled someone
on the other team.

Sure enough, Grandma was coming down the sideline toward us doing backflips.

"Go, Ethan!" she shouted. "You know what to do!"

And I did! I got the ball and imagined myself on a zip line. I zipped past the other team so fast, their shorts blew off.

Two guys tried to block me, but I did a karate move and they ran into each other.

There was only one more person between me and the goal. . . . He was big. And mean.

"Give me the ball or I'll crush you!" he said with a sneer.

I tripped, then flipped upside down and kicked the soccer ball in midair. (I'm not sure, but I think it was in slow motion.)

"Hey, no fair!" he shouted.

But by then the ball had sailed past him and past the goalie. It hit the back of the net so hard it deflated.

"Score!" yelled the referee. He blew his whistle.
We won!

My teammates were like, *"Whoa!"* They carried me off the field on their shoulders. (Only for a second. Mom made them put me down.)

That night at bedtime Mom and Dad told me how proud they were.

"I'm proud of you too," said a voice from the doorway.

"Grandma!" I said. "I'm sorry I told you not to be a ninja!"
"No," said Grandma. "I'm through being a ninja anyway."

"What?" I cried. "You're just going to be a regular old grandma?"
"I didn't say that," she said.

"I'm going to be a pirate instead."